Leroy

The Smallest Elf of All

Story by Robert Barfield

Illustrated by Jessica Smith

I suppose that children all over the world have heard of the North Pole where Santa Claus lives; and where all of his elves build all of the toys that girls and boys receive for Christmas. But, I wonder, how many children have heard yet about Leroy, the smallest elf of all?

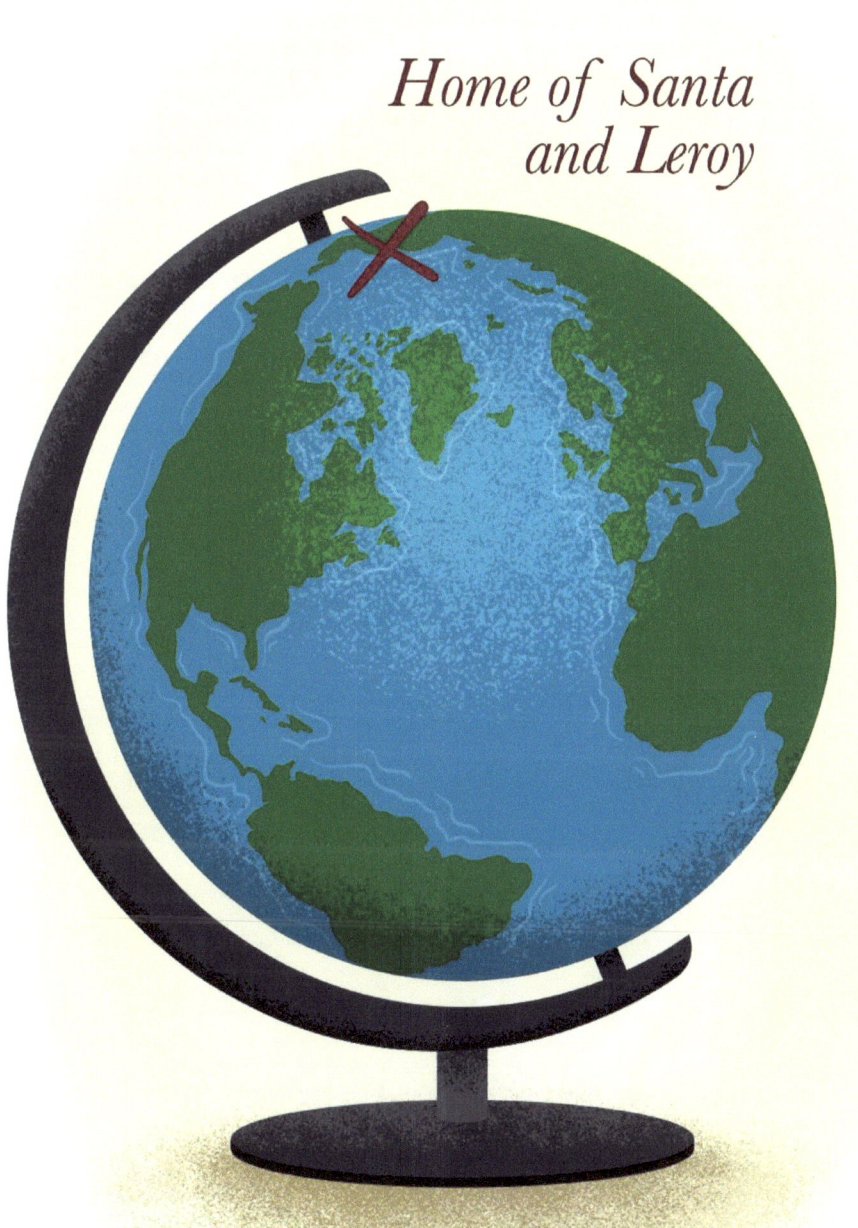

Home of Santa and Leroy

Well, not too long ago, when the snow was falling and you could tell by all the excitement in the air that Christmas was near; Santa and Mrs. Claus had just finished their lunch when Mrs. Claus noticed that Santa had hardly eaten any of his food and seemed to be very worried about something.

"Santa", she said, "why you have hardly eaten enough to fill a bird; are you feeling ill?" "No dear" said Santa, "I might as well tell you. I've been trying to lose a lot of weight; and I've been very worried lately." "Whatever for?" said Mrs. Claus. "Because of all the new houses that are being built" said Santa.

"They seem to be making the chimneys smaller and smaller. Why some of the houses just have pipes sticking out of the roofs for chimneys. Electric heaters I guess, I don't know how in the world I'll be able to climb down those things, unless I lose an awful lot of weight in a hurry."

Too worried
to eat

Mrs. Claus could see that Santa was really troubled, so to take his mind off of things she said to him, "Santa, why don't you go over to the workshop and see how the elves are coming along with all the Christmas toys? It is really snowing hard and Christmas Eve will soon be here. When you get back I'll have some hot chocolate waiting for you and a nice piece of hot apple pie. We can't have you not eating! You might get sick. You've got a lot of toys to deliver soon and you'll need your strength."

So, Santa bundled up in his jacket, put on his boots and cap and walked through the snow over to his workshop.

When Santa opened the door to his workshop and walked in, what a bunch of busy little elves he saw! There were elves hammering here, sawing over there, some were sewing, some were polishing; doing just about anything you could think of to build toys. All of the elves had their own work benches, some long, some short, but all about the same height.

Busy little elves

As Santa was walking around the toy shop looking to see how much more work needed to be done, he thought he heard a noise like someone crying. "Can't be", said Santa out loud; "it must be a saw that someone is using." But as he turned around, he saw Leroy, the smallest elf of all the elves all by himself.

Now, no one knows for sure how small an elf really is; but we do know that Leroy was the smallest elf of all. Sitting in a corner of the shop near a big pile of sawdust was Leroy. There were tears running down his cheeks and he was crying. Santa walked over to Leroy, picked

Why are
you crying?

him up gently and said, "My word Leroy, this is one of the happiest places in the entire world. Why are you crying?"

"Oh Santa", said Leroy, " I am so small I can't reach the work benches even if I stand on a box, so all I can do is sweep the floors and run errands for all of the other elves." Then Santa told Leroy how important his job was. He told him that the other elves couldn't do their work without him because no one wants to work in a sloppy dirty shop. Leroy said "I know that Santa, but I never have a chance to make children happy by building toys for Christmas."

*All **I** do is clean*

Santa took out his handkerchief and wiped away Leroy's tears and told him not to worry that he would think of something else for Leroy to do. As Santa walked off, he thought to himself. "Poor little Leroy, he is very small and the other elves are so busy they hardly have time to notice him."

Suddenly, Santa got an Idea that made him stop right where he was. Laying his finger aside of his nose he thought for a minute. "Umm, that's it!" he said to himself. "I'll ask Mrs. Claus if she can make Leroy a little Santa suit and then I can take him with me on Christmas Eve. Why the Chimneys that are too small for me, Little Leroy could whisk right down in nothing flat."

Santa ran all the way back to his house he was so excited. When he opened the door he scooped Mrs. Claus into his arms and danced with her around the kitchen. "My goodness", said Ms. Claus. "Why are you so excited? He told Mrs. Claus all about little Leroy and the idea he had about taking Leroy with him on Christmas Eve. "Wonderful", she said. "Leroy will be happy and you won't have to starve yourself and you will eat like you should. I'll start right now and have a suit for little Leroy in no time at all!"

Well, I don't know where you would ever find a lady anywhere who could sew any faster or any better than Mrs. Claus, and by the time you can say Merry Christmas and Happy New Year three times, Leroy's suit was finished, with a little Santa cap and even some black boots.

Ready in
no time at all.

"I just can't wait to show these to Leroy and tell him of my idea", said Santa, and he rushed out of the house, ran through the snow back to his workshop.

"Stop your work, stop your work" he shouted, as he ran into the shop. "Where is Leroy?" Naturally all of the other elves were wondering what in the world Santa wanted Leroy for and they soon found out. "What is it Santa?" Leroy said as he rushed to where Santa was standing.

Santa told Leroy all about his idea; how he needed him just in case he came across a chimney that was too small for him to get down. He showed Leroy the little Santa suit that Mrs. Claus had made for him and you can just guess how happy Leroy was that day, and I guess it would be safe to say that not only was Leroy the smallest elf of all but, also, the happiest elf of all.

Santa's
helper

So remember, the next time you boys and girls look up at your roof and wonder how Santa Claus will be able to get down into your house, just think of the story about little Leroy. And, don't be surprised, that is if you're lucky enough; and have a very small chimney, to see Leroy in your living room on Christmas Eve.

Whoops!

The End

Merry Christmas

www.ingramcontent.com/pod-product-compliance
Lightning Source LLC
Chambersburg PA
CBHW040901120626
46551CB00001B/120